# MY LiFe
## as a
### Stupendously
# STOMPED
# Soccer Star

the incredible worlds of **Wally M<sup>c</sup>Doogle**

MY LiFe
as a
Stupendously
STOMPED
Soccer Star

# BILL MYERS

NELSON

**A Division of Thomas Nelson Publishers**

NASHVILLE  DALLAS  MEXICO CITY  RIO DE JANEIRO

Published in Nashville, Tennessee, by Tommy Nelson. Tommy Nelson is
a registered trademark of Thomas Nelson, Inc.

Tommy Nelson books may be purchased in bulk for educational,
business, fund-raising, or sales promotional use. For information,
please email SpecialMarkets@ThomasNelson.com.

Scripture quotations in this book are from the *International Children's
Bible®*, *New Century Version®*, © 1986, 1988, 1999 by Tommy Nelson®, a
Division of Thomas Nelson, Inc. All rights reserved.

### Library of Congress Cataloging-in-Publication Data

Myers, Bill, 1953–
    My life as a stupendously stomped soccer star / Bill Myers.
      p. cm.— (The incredible worlds of Wally McDoogle ; 26)
    Summary: Enabled by an overactive imagination to make his every
wish come true, Wally becomes the world's greatest soccer player,
but he soon realizes that God's plans for himself and the world may
be better than his own.
    ISBN: 978-1-4003-0635-0 (trade paper)
    [1. Wishes—Fiction. 2. Christian life—Fiction. 3. Athletes—
Fiction. 4. Soccer—Fiction. 5. Humorous stories.] I. Title. II. Series:
Myers, Bill, 1953– . Incredible worlds of Wally McDoogle ; #26.
PZ7.M98234Myle 2006
[Fic]—dc22

                        2006004471

*Printed in the United States of America*

10 11 12 13 14 EPAC 9 8 7 6 5 4

"Give thanks whatever happens."

—1 Thessalonians 5:18

For Sonny Cruise:
A genius in his own right.

# Contents

# Chapter 1

## Just for Starters

It all began simply enough—which should have been my first clue we were heading for trouble (at least in these books).

I was at soccer tryouts being my incredible, nonathletic self. This, of course, involved the usual number of

—torn muscles,
—sprained ankles, and
—broken body parts.

As the world's "Master of Disaster" (I hold a fifth-degree black belt in self-destruction), this was nothing new. What was new was that most of it was brought on by one Sophie Stompuregut.

I don't want to say Sophie is tough, but she's the only soccer player I know who is required to wear a sign on the back of her uniform reading:

1

CAUTION: The Surgeon General has determined that playing me can be hazardous to your health.

So there we were, out on the soccer field showing our stuff, when I made three major mistakes:

1. I accidentally got into the clear.
2. I shouted, "I'm open, pass to me, pass to me!"

And number three? Actually, that's before I got onto the field. That's when . . .

3. I actually thought I'd try out for a sport.

I know, I know, talk about brain-dead. I should have known better. But Wall Street had been so convincing:

"Come on," she had said. "You'll do great. I'll be your sports agent, and we'll make a ton of money." (Wall Street wants to make her first million by the time she's fifteen. Most of it off me.)

"How can we make money if we spend it all on hospital bills?" I demanded.

"There won't be any hospital bills," she argued.

"Okay, funeral bills."

"There won't be any of those, either."

"Are you sure?" I asked.

"Trust me," she said, grinning.

Which, of course, was another mistake (I know I said there were three, but I've never been good at math):

4. I trusted Wall Street.

I figured I was in trouble when I arrived at the field and saw her yelling through a megaphone:

"Step right up! See the world's greatest klutz in action. Hear his screams of torture, his gasps of agony, the cracking of his breaking bones. Buy your tickets now while he's still alive!"

Good ol' Wall Street.

Anyway, so there I was out on the field, shouting for the ball, when the forward saw I was in the clear and passed to me.

I expertly trapped it (hey, accidents happen) and started up field. That's when I spotted Sophie bearing down on me.

Unfortunately, she had one of those I-haven't-killed-a-player-in-a-good-two-minutes-and-I'm-getting-kinda-cranky looks on her face.

No problem. I immediately started to use all my athletic skills (which, unfortunately, *was* a problem).

I faked right, then left, then right.

Sophie slowed to a stop and watched as I continued faking this way and that, that way and this. Actually, I was really getting pretty good at it. Of course, I hadn't moved up field an inch, but I was sure impressing myself.

Unfortunately, I wasn't impressing Sophie. After a few more minutes of boredom, she went for the ball (which also involved smashing her very sharp forearm into my very soft face).

I tried shouting, "Foul! Foul!" But it's hard shouting anything when your mouth has been knocked to the back of your head.

It's harder still when you're suddenly

*K-Wham!*

slide-tackled . . .

*K-Thud!*

to the ground and have

> *squish-squish-squish*
> "Ouch! Ouch! Ouch!"

some supertough girl running up and down your back with some supersharp cleats.

But that was nothing compared to that same girl accidentally mistaking my head for a soccer ball (at least, I thought it was an accident) and accidentlier

*K-BAMB*ing

it as hard as she could.

The good news was, they did *NOT* count it a point when my body flew past the goalie and into the net.

The bad news was, I didn't have time to celebrate. It's hard to celebrate anything when you're busy losing consciousness.

\* \* \* \* \*

When I woke up things were whiter than a marshmallow lost in a blizzard inside a bottle of liquid whiteout. Seriously, the place was almost as white as the sheets Mom puts on the guest bed whenever Grandma sleeps over.

"Hello?" I shouted. "Is anybody here?"

"I'm always here," a voice replied.

I looked in every direction but could see only white. "Where are you?" I shouted. "Where am I?"

"I think you know where you are," the voice replied.

I swallowed. "Am I . . . in heaven?"

"Sorry, Wally, you're not in heaven."

I took a bigger swallow. "Then am I in . . . the other place?"

"Don't be ridiculous," the voice answered. "You don't see anyone around here having to eat your little sister's cooking, do you?"

"They do that in the other place?"

"Can you think of any worse torture?"

He had a point.

"No, don't worry," the voice said. "You're simply in one of your I'm-unconscious-from-one-too-many-disasters states. You'll eventually wake up."

I nodded and tried swallowing again. But there was something about the voice that made my mouth drier than sand baked at 350 degrees for seven hours in the desert—(which can also be mistaken for my little sister Carrie's lima-bean casserole).

"Are you . . . God?" I croaked.

"Don't be ridiculous."

"Then who—"

"I'm just your overactive imagination representing God."

I frowned. "What does that mean?"

"It means you have a problem with the way God is running things, and together we're going to straighten it out."

"I don't have a problem with God," I argued. "Well, except for making me too short, too clumsy, too stupid, too ugly, too unlucky, too clumsy—"

"You said 'clumsy' already."

"I did? Okay, then add too clueless, too non-athletic, and way too clumsy. Other than that, I'm just fine."

"You're sure?"

"Absolutely . . . well, other than being a little too clumsy."

"I see. And if you had the chance to be God, you would change that?"

"In a heartbeat! In half a heartbeat! In half of a half of a heart—"

"Hold it," the voice interrupted. "Overactive imaginations aren't great with fractions. But I get your point."

The voice paused a moment as if thinking. Finally, it answered, "Okay . . . done."

"Done what?"

"You can change it."

"Change what?"

"Anything you want."

"Are you serious?!"

"Absolutely. For the next few days I'll change whatever you ask."

"Wow!" I cried. "Just like the genie in the bottle story!"

"Actually"—he cleared his throat—"as an overactive imagination, I'm good enough not to borrow other people's stories."

"Sorry."

"Each change you decide to make will go into effect at midnight. But remember, once you've made them, they will remain permanent. Is that clear?"

"You bet! That's way cooler than some stupid genie in a bottle."

"My point exactly. And your first change will be?"

"What, now? You're ready to start now?!"

"Absolutely. It'll be midnight in a few minutes. What change would you like to make for tomorrow?"

"This is incredible!"

I couldn't believe it. My mind spun, my heart raced, my breath, er, breathed, until I finally shouted, "I've got it!"

"And it is?"

"I want to be the country's greatest soccer player!"

"Then, starting at midnight, you will become the country's greatest soccer star. Good luck."

"Thanks!"

"You'll be needing it . . ."

# Chapter 2

## Wally McDoogle:
## Stupendous Something-or-Other

I opened my eyes and stared at the ceiling. Then I rolled over in bed to stare at my alarm clock. It read:

$$11:37$$

Of course, I knew that whole thing about my "overactive imagination" was just a dream (although a very overactive one). So, of course, I wasn't taking it seriously.

Still, with nothing else to do except count the number of bones Sophie had broken at soccer tryouts (hey, everybody needs a hobby), I decided to stay awake, just in case.

To kill time, I reached for Ol' Betsy, my faithful laptop computer, and started another one of my superhero stories . . .

It had been another long day of superherodom for our supersized superhero...Pudgy Boy.

Already he had battled the fiendishly foul Fad Diet Dude—that skinny slimeball who convinced the world that a steady diet of slugs was the key to quick weight loss.

(And he was right...if you count the number of times per day it made people hurl.)

## Rubber Band Workout Machine
## as advertised on TV.

After that came his fight with Rubber Band Man. The sinister stretcher was selling his revolutionary *Rubber Band Workout Machine as advertised on TV.* You've seen the commercials—just 99 payments of $99 for 99 months will buy your very own rubber band to stretch back and forth between your fingers. What better way to burn off those unwanted fractions of a calorie?

But now, at last, his day is over. He flops down in his Fat Cave and is

about to order his usual deluxe pizza
with extra caramel sauce and chocolate
chip topping (how else do you think
he got so pudgy?) when, suddenly, the
Flab Phone

*Blubber-Blubber-Blubber*
*Blubber-Blubber-Blubber*

rings. He reaches for it and answers:

"Pudgy Boy here:
If bad guys give you
eating disorders,
In prison, I'll make them
permanent boarders."
(Hey, he's a superhero, not a superpoet.)

"Pudgy Boy!" a voice shouts from the other end of the phone. "This is a national emergency!"

"Mr. President! Is this you?"

"Of course it's me, who else would be calling you at the beginning of these superhero stories!"

"But you sound so different! Your
voice, it's somehow...thinner."

"Look out your window, and I'll explain!"

Our roly-poly hero rolls out of his
chair and waddles to the window.

Outside, the road is covered with all sorts of people exercising. Everyone is jogging, skipping rope, running in place, doing jumping jacks.

And not just a little, but a lot. Crazily. Desperately. They are drenched in sweat and so exhausted they can barely stand. Still, they keep pushing themselves as they do sit-ups, push-ups, and (with all that exercising, what else) throw-ups.

"What's going on?" our hero cries.

"It's the fiendish work of your archenemy...Boney Boy."

"Don't tell me he's created more of those belly-baring fashions that you have to have a perfect body to wear?"

"Worse than that! He's manipulating people's brain waves——making everyone want to get thinner and thinner and thinner some more."

"Is that why everyone's exercising so hard?"

"Yes! Everyone hates themselves for not having superthin bodies. But it's not just bodies. Butchers are slicing their meat thinner. TV screens are becoming thinner. Even iPods——"

"Your voice! Mr. President, is that what's happening to your voice?"

"Yes! Everything's getting thinner! Hurry Pudgy Boy! You're the only one who can save us! You're the only who..."

"Mr. President, I can barely hear you. Mr. President, please try to speak a little fatter."

With great effort, the President tries again. "Hurry, Pudgy Boy. Before we become nothing but..."

"Mr. President! Mr. President!!"
But there is no answer.

In desperation, Pudgy Boy lets out a loud but incredibly thin

"Great Scott!" he shouts. "It's even happening to me!"

In a surge of superhero strength, he waddles through the Fat Cave to do what he has to do while there's still time for him to do it.

### TRANSLATION:
Better hold off on that pizza till
the world gets saved...

I stopped for a moment and glanced at the clock. It now read:

12:02

Of course, nothing had happened. How could it? It was just my overactive imagination being overactively imaginative (imagine that).

*Oh well,* I thought as I shut Ol' Betsy down and slid under the covers. *Everything can't always go the way you want it.* Of course, I'd settle for anything going any way I want it, but some things aren't meant to be.

Little did I know how wrong I was . . .

* * * * *

"Mista McDoogla, wake up!"

I tried opening my eyes, but they were heavier than my little cousin's diapers when it's my uncle's turn to watch him.

"Mista McDoogla!"

The voice was no longer just talking. Now it was dragging me

*K-Thud*

out of bed and down the

*K-bamb—thump!*
*K-bamb—thump!*
*K-bamb—thump!*

stairs.

The good news was, all that *K-bamb*ing and *K-thump*ing had finally jarred my eyes open. The bad news was, I suddenly started to

> *chatter-chatter-chatter*
> *chatter-chatter-chatter,*

which, of course, is the sound my teeth make when I'm dragged outside at 3:30 in the morning in my underwear!

I staggered to my feet and looked up to see a giant muscleman climbing onto a motorbike.

"Who are, *chatter-chatter-chatter,* you?!" I shouted.

"I am yar pursanal trainer, Arnold S'poseta Nag-v!"

"What??"

"No time to talk. Time iz vaisting!"

Before I could chatter more protests (or at least come down with a good case of pneumonia), he fired up his motorbike, put it into gear, and

## *V-ROOOM*Med

directly at me.

I leaped out of the way, nearly becoming a permanent part of his tire tread.

"What are you doing?!" I screamed.

He spun the bike back around to face me. "You cannot raymain de number one soccer player in de coundry ef you don't vurk out! Now run!"

"What?!"

Again he

# V-R*OOO*MMed

toward me, and again I leaped out of the way.

"Run!" he shouted as he spun the bike back around. "You mus run!"

I got the picture and started jogging down the driveway.

He pulled up behind me, his front tire just inches from my

# V-R*OOO*MM V-R*OOO*MM

rear.

"Fasta, girlie boy! Fasta!"

I turned left onto the street. He followed right behind.

"Fasta! Fasta!"

Now, you didn't have to be a genius to figure out what had happened. I had become the number one soccer player in the country, and this was my daily workout session!

How cool was that?! My wish had actually come true!

Of course, it would have been cooler if I'd remembered to wear shoes, a few more clothes, and was actually in shape. But after fifteen or so miles of

### V-R*OOO*MM V-R*OOO*MM
"Fasta! Fasta!"
*pant-pant, wheeze-wheeze, die-die,*

the fun and games finally came to an end.

Well, maybe the fun . . . but by the looks of things, the games had just begun. Next stop was . . .

**OUR KITCHEN**

Mom wasn't up yet, but I guess that didn't matter. Arnie was also my dietician.

I'd barely regained consciousness from our little gasp-a-thon before he made a delicious breakfast of raw eggs, curdled yak milk, and a half quart of stewed cauliflower.

Of course, I tried to leave (before I heaved), but that would have involved moving my legs, which still had no feeling since my jogging workout.

Anyway, he slammed the delicious mixture onto the counter in front of me and grinned.

I tried to protest. "But—"

"Opan up!"

"But—but—"

"Opan up, girlie boy!"

"But—but—but—"

Before I could impress him with any more of my astonishing logic, he stomped on my foot, which suddenly had feeling, which suddenlier made me open my mouth to scream.

But, of course, no scream came. It's hard to scream when you're chugging down raw eggs, curdled yak milk, and stewed cauliflower.

I don't want to say it tasted bad, but at the moment I'd have given anything to wash it down with some of my little sister's cooking.

But that was only the beginning. Next stop was . . .

## SCHOOL

I don't want to say people acted differently because I was a famous athlete, but it was a little embarrassing when everyone treated me like some sort of celebrity (with the IQ of a cockroach).

Take Mr. Brainboredom's English class. He went around the whole room having everyone read a few paragraphs from *Julia's Seizures* (or whatever that Shakespeare play is called). But when it got to be my turn, he said, "That's okay, Wally, you don't have to."

"But I want to."

"No, really, we don't want you to strain yourself."

"Strain myself?"

"Well, yeah, you know—having to use your brain and everything."

"You think just because I'm an athlete I don't have a brain?"

"It's nothing to be embarrassed about."

"Come on," I insisted. "Let me read something. I'll show you."

"Well, okay then. Read the top of the page. Way up in the right-hand corner. Do you see it?"

"You mean where the page number is?"

"That's right. And what does it say?"

"43?"

"Very good." Mr. Brainboredom began to clap. "Class, let's hear it for Wally."

Before I knew it, everybody was giving me a standing ovation.

Unfortunately, there was plenty more weirdness to follow in . . .

## THE HALLWAY

It was the custom in our school that whenever jocks passed one another, they gave high-fives.

Unfortunately, it was no different with me.

"Hey, McDoogle!"—*K-Slap!*
"What's up, man?!"—*K-Pow!*
"How's it going?!"—*K-Bamb!*

Actually, it was pretty cool, and I wouldn't have minded it except for all my broken wrists, broken arms, and other structural damage.

Finally, there were . . .

## MY FRIENDS

I knew Opera and Wall Street wouldn't treat me differently. After all, we'd been friends ever since Camp Wahkah-Wahkah.

I finally spotted them in the cafeteria line (better known as the death row). Wall Street was trying to sell nose plugs so you couldn't taste the food, and Opera was busy listening to classical music through headphones that were surgically implanted into his ears.

"Hey, guys!" I shouted.

It was about this time that Opera turned, saw me, and immediately

"YIKES!"

ran for his life.

How weird was that?

Figuring he mistook me for someone else, I grabbed a tray and filled it up with the usual culinary delights of crusted-over spaghetti, crusted-over Jell-O, and crusted-over apple juice.

I then strolled on over to join Opera and Wall Street at our table. We call it "our table" 'cause it's way off in the corner, all by itself, so no one will accidentally sit with us.

Not that we blamed them for setting us apart. Until the tests come back to prove you can't catch dorkiness by sitting too close to a Dorkoid, everyone is careful to keep their distance.

"Hey, guys," I repeated as I sat down beside Opera.

He looked at me and suddenly did an encore performance of

## "YIKES!"

But this time he leaped to his feet and ran out of the room.

"What's with him?" I asked Wall Street.

She looked at me and frowned. "You're a jock."

"Meaning . . ."

"Meaning you're required by law to be a bully."

"I'm no bully."

"Yeah, right," she said scornfully. "The point is, it's been over a week since Opera has been thrown into the showers or has had his head dunked into a toilet."

"So?"

"So, he's due."

"And he thinks I'll do it?" I asked.

"Why else would you come over to our table?"

"To be your friend?"

"Get real," she said, scooping up her own tray and also moving off.

"Hey, where you going?" I cried.

"Jocks don't sit with Dorkoids. You know that."

"But—"

"Go hang out with your musclebound mutants and quit terrorizing the rest of us." With that, she was gone.

Suddenly, I was sitting all by myself and feeling very much alone.

No matter how you figure it, things hadn't turned out so well. Little did I realize that this not-so-wellness was nothing compared to the unwellness that was about to come.

### TRANSLATION:
Buckle in, sports fans.
It's going to get a lot worse.

# Chapter 3

## Almost... but Not Quite

Luckily, soccer tryouts went a little better than school.

Of course, there was the problem of all the beautiful babes fighting over who was going to carry my books to the locker room . . .

"You got to carry his science book the last fifteen feet. It's my turn!"

"But you got to carry his notebook *and* his math book!"

And don't even get me started on the girls who were too busy fainting over my presence to do much of anything—except clutter up the hallway.

Suiting up in the locker room was just as cool.

"Hey, Wally, will you sign my shoes?"

"Hey, Wally, will you sign my T-shirt?"

"Hey, Wally, will you sign my undershorts?"

Then there was Coach Hurtumuch:

"Okay, men, listen up. We're honored that the great Wally McDoogle has chosen to try out for our team."

This was followed by the usual clapping, cheering, and standing ovations.

The coach continued. "However, I promise you that there will be no favoritism. Lord McDoogle will be treated like everybody else . . . just as soon as the limo takes him onto the field and he's had his personal sauna, massage, and manicure."

This, of course, was followed by more clapping, cheering, and underwear signing until I finally entered the limo and headed to the field.

Now, I don't want to brag, but as a soccer player, I was sensational, remarkable, incredible (and any other *ible* word you can imagine). It's hard to explain, but just imagine living in a world where everything is backward. A world where

—people *give* gifts on their birthdays,
—politicians can be trusted,
—everything I do doesn't backfire.

After we divided up into teams and started playing, I was unstoppable. Of course, Sophie Stompuregut tried checking me, but she'd have been more helpful if she'd have just gone off to the movies.

Granted, I was moving a little slow in the first period (scoring only 27 points), but there's just so much time on the clock for one person to dribble all the way down the field and score again and again . . . and again some more.

Only after the first period ended did Coach suggest we try a different strategy.

"Lord McDoogle?"

I chose to give him a thrill by looking in his direction.

"Would you mind passing the ball off once in a while? Just to keep things interesting?"

It sounded like a novel idea, so in the second period I did just that . . .

I got the ball, triple-faked Sophie, and passed to our team captain, Stanley Superjoke.

Now, I don't want to say ol' Stan was bad, but other words like *awful, terrible*, and *embarrassing* do come to mind. (In short, he was only ten times better than I used to be.) In fact, he was moving so slow that I raced ahead of the ball, jumped, and gave it a header up the field.

Unfortunately, the next teammate, Wynona Wannabeaplayer, was no better.

So, with no one else to turn to, I outmaneuvered Sophie, passed the ball, raced ahead of it, and gave it one of my famous triple-whammy bicycle kicks to . . . who else but me, who dribbled

it down the field, passed it off to . . . me, who
dribbled it, passed it to . . . me, who went in and
kicked it for a point! (Coach was right, passing
the ball did make things a lot more interesting.)

And so the game continued. Me passing it to
me, who passed it to me, who headed it to me,
who . . . well, you get the picture.

Then, when things got boring, I started playing the goalie as well.

Yes sir, the good news was, the rest of the
team could take the day off and join Sophie at
the movies. Who needed eleven players when
there was one wonderful Wally McDoogle, superstar.

The bad news was, for some reason, some of
my teammates got a little jealous. Can you imagine, one or two actually accused me of being a
ball hog?

It got so bad that by the end of the third
period when the score was 1,234 to 1 (they got
the 1 because I had to take a restroom break),
nobody on my team remained on the field.
They'd all gone home.

Including Coach. (I forgot to mention that in
the last minutes I'd been playing his position as
well.)

I felt a little bad . . . and a lot lonely. It was
worse than being deserted by Wall Street and

Opera in the cafeteria. Now I didn't have anybody to call friend. Not my fellow Dorkoids, not
my fellow players.

Nobody.

Talk about weird. I'd gotten everything I'd
wanted, but somehow things were worse than
before.

But that's okay. Midnight would be rolling
around in a few hours. I'd just ask for things to
go back to what they used to be.

A piece of cake, right?

No sweat . . . no problem . . .

And, as you've already guessed . . . no way.

I got home and dragged my body up the
stairs. (Even the country's greatest soccer star
can get tuckered out.)

Of course, Mom was worried that I didn't
want dinner. The fact that she'd cooked pot roast
and carrots made it more than a little tempting.
But I'd been busier than an Oompa-Loompa in a
Wonka chocolate factory. In fact, my head had
barely hit the pillow before I drifted off and my
imagination started working again.

\* \* \* \* \*

"Hey there, Wally."
I opened my eyes and saw a giant horse

standing on my bed looking down at me. This, of course, inspired me to practice my world-famous and ever-popular

"AUGH!"

as I grabbed my pillow and leaped under the covers, praying for my life.

"Come on, Wally, knock it off."

"M-m-mees m-m-mwont eet m-mwe!"

(That's supposed to be "P-p-please d-d-don't eat m-m-me," but it's hard begging for your life when you're screaming into a pillow.)

"Come on, Wally, knock it off. It's me."

"M-mwe mwho?"

"Me, your overactive imagination."

Ever so slowly, I pulled the covers off of my head.

The horse gave a little whinny and shook his mane.

I gave a major scream and dove back under the covers.

"Wally . . ."

I felt his lips grab the covers and pull them back farther and farther until it was just me lying there in my Fruit of the Looms. I finally looked up to stare directly into his giant, flaring nostrils.

With my last ounce of courage, I managed to stutter, "Wh-what happened to the white room and th-the voice?"

"Oh, please. What self-respecting imagination would do the same thing twice? Hey, did you check out my cool wings?" He dropped his shoulder so I could see two giant white wings fluttering on his back.

I nodded. The wings were very impressive. Though I'd have preferred being impressed with him as a parakeet or a ladybug or just about anything else that didn't tower seven feet over my bed smelling like oats.

"Am I . . ." I took another breath and gave it another try. "Am I asleep, again?"

"Yeah, probably," he said. "So how was your day? Was it everything you'd hoped?"

I nodded. "And worse."

He gave a snort, which I guess is how horses say, "I told you so."

"It really wasn't that bad," I argued. "In fact, it was pretty cool. It was just . . . well, it wasn't as cool as I thought it would be."

"It never is."

"So if you just let me change things back to—"

"No, that was the deal, remember? You can't change anything back."

"Oh yeah." I frowned. "I forgot."

"See, that's what I was trying to tell you. God always knows what's best. You just have to trust—"

"No, wait a minute! I've got something."

He sighed wearily as he reached his long neck down to the backpack next to my bed.

"What are you doing?" I asked.

"Just checking for sugar cubes."

"Sorry. Listen, I have an idea. You say I can't change anything back, right?"

"Right."

"I can't change things back . . . but I can add things on. That's what you said, right? As long as it's before midnight, I can add new things."

"Yes . . ."

I sat up straighter in bed. "Okay, this is what I want. I don't want to be the country's greatest soccer player, I want to be the world's greatest player."

"I knew that was coming."

"And I want Opera and Wall Street to still be my best friends."

His eyes widened. "But they're Dorkoids."

"So."

"So you'll be a superjock. The two never hang together."

"Are you saying this is too big for an over-active imagination?"

He snorted in contempt. "Believe me, I can imagine anything you throw at me."

"Good. Then that's what I want. I'm still a star soccer player . . . but they're still my friends!"

"All right," he said, sighing. "If that's what you want."

I folded my arms in triumph. "That's what I want. Oh, and tell Arnie boy I'm taking tomorrow off."

"All right . . ." I didn't like the sound of his voice as he climbed off my bed. "Then so be it."

"That's it?" I asked.

"Of course," he said, sighing as he started for the door.

"Wait a minute, where are you going?"

"Is that cooked carrots I smell downstairs?"

"Left over from dinner, yeah."

"Great." He took another step, then he suddenly stopped and turned. "Tonight wasn't Carrie's turn to cook, was it?"

"Nah, that was last night."

He smiled and continued out the door, clip-clopping down the hall and toward the stairs.

I thought of warning Mom and Dad (something about a horse strolling through your living room in the middle of *Jeopardy* might be a little startling). Then again, they've got their own imaginations. Let them deal with it.

I, on the other hand, was expecting to enjoy some incredible things.

But, as usual, my expecter wasn't exactly expecting to get what it expected when it was expecting it . . .

### TRANSLATION:

Aw, never mind . . . you'll find out soon enough.

# Chapter 4

## Another Day,

## Another Billion (or Two)

The next day, as my chauffeur stopped in front of school (how else would the world's greatest soccer player get there?), I climbed out of the hot tub, dried off, walked past the juice bar, home theater system, and tennis courts, and finally stepped out of my super **S—T—R—E—T—C—H** limo (what else would a SUPERjock ride in?).

There to meet me was Opera. Good ol' Opera.

Only he wasn't quite as good or ol' as before. Oh, he still had his headphones permanently attached to his ears, and he was no doubt still listening to his opera music, but there were definitely a few changes.

First, there was his black suit, black shirt, and black tie. (The only time I'd seen him in a tie was when we had a toilet-side funeral service for my goldfish.)

Then there was his size. He'd put on a few extra pounds.

Actually, a lot of extra pounds. Actually, he looked like King Kong on steroids!

Finally, there was the way he spoke:

"Godfather Wally, *burp*—" (Opera always burps. It's something about all the candy, cookies, and chips he puts down.) "I am honored dat yas have chosen me and da boys to protect yas from yas, *burp*, enemies."

I frowned. "Why are you talking so funny?"

"I am honored dat yas have noticed." He grinned as he pulled out a book from his back pocket titled:

How to Talk Like a
Big-Time Thug and Bodyguard

"Bodyguard?" I asked. "What do I need a bodyguard for?"

"To protect yas from all yas, *burp*, enemies."

"What?"

Without answering, he grabbed my shoulders, leaned forward, and gave me a kiss on one cheek,

"Eeeew . . ."

and then the other.

Double "Eeeew . . ."

His burper breath freaked me out. I don't
want to say it was bad, but he'd just finished
his seventeenth bag of **Hot 'N Spicey Garlic
Chips** and I noticed the frames of my glasses
had started to melt.

"You said 'enemies'?" I coughed as I waved
aside the toxic vapors. "What enemies?"

He motioned over his shoulder just as a
fourth grader came running toward me with a
pencil and paper. "Mr. McDoogle, can I have
your autograph? Will you sign my—"

But that's all he got out before Opera's fingers
snapped.

Suddenly, a half-dozen goons, bigger than
the Incredible Hulk on a grumpy day, grabbed
the kid and started dragging him off.

"Mr. McDoogle!" the kid yelled. "Help me!
Help me!"

"What are you doing?" I shouted at Opera.
"Where are you taking him?"

"Why, to da lavatory, of course."

"The lavatory?"

"Where else can we turn him upside down,
dunk his head in da toilet, and flush it?"

"But that's what the bullies used to do to
you!" I cried.

"Not no more," he said, burping.

I couldn't believe my ears. What had happened to Opera's kindness (let alone his good grammar)?

"But it's wrong!" I shouted. "What you're doing is terrible!"

"Not as terrible as dis."

He snapped his fingers at a handful of second graders who were running toward me, their cute little faces filled with smiles and excitement.

Well, their faces had been filled with smiles and excitement. But that was before another half-dozen bodyguards appeared, yanked them up by the backs of their underwear, and hung them on nearby tree limbs.

"Help us!" they shouted, kicking and screaming. "Get us down, get us down!"

"Look!" Opera said, laughing menacingly. "Christmas tree ornaments!"

"What are you doing?" I demanded. I raced to the tree to help the kids down. "What made you turn so mean?!"

"I'm friends of da great Wally McDoogle," he said, grinning. "I can do anything I want."

"Yeah, but—"

"Children shudder at my presence, bullies drop to der knees, and teachers—"

Suddenly, he spotted our principal stepping out of his office.

"Hey," Opera yelled. "What did I tell yas 'bout coming outside without my permission?!'

The principal looked up, his eyes widening in fear. "I'm so sorry, Mr. Opera, I didn't—"

"What did yas call me?!"

"I'm sorry . . . *O Great One*. I simply forgot."

"Save yas excuses. Get back inside and order me another truckload of dem **Hot 'N Spicey Garlic Chips**."

"Yes, O Great One."

"And another boxcar of Chippy Chipper potato chips. I'm down to my last crate."

(Well, now I understood how he'd gained the extra tonnage.)

He turned to me and began an evil laugh

"Moo-hoo-hoo . . ."

that grew louder,

"Haa-haa-haa . . ."

and louder some more:

"Haar-haar-harr . . ."

It was amazing. But by remaining my close friend after I'd become famous, Opera had completely changed. He was entirely different from—

"*Burp!* Hey, dat was a good one."

Well, maybe not entirely different, but different enough. And none of it was good.

Unfortunately, he wasn't the only one who had changed. Because, suddenly, there was a brand-new

*Whop-Whop-Whop-Whop*

sound effect.

Opera and I looked up to see a sleek, jet-powered helicopter dropping from the clouds.

Kids were running back and forth, yelling and screaming as it set down on the school's lawn. The door slid open, and who should step out but . . .Wall Street.

Well, I thought it was Wall Street. It was hard to tell with the sunglasses, briefcase, power-business suit, and high heels. Then, of course, there was the cell phone she had to her ear.

"No, no, no!" she shouted into the phone. "He's on David Letterman that night."

"Hey, Wall Street," I called.

She gave a nod but continued shouting into the phone. "No, then he's starring in a Flex Pecs bodybuilding commercial. No, after that he's having dinner with the Pope!"

I nervously glanced at Opera.

Wall Street continued shouting into the phone. "Tell him to stop being a baby. He'll just have to wait in line to meet the great Wally McDoogle like everyone else. Good-bye!" Angrily, she snapped off the phone.

"Who was dat?" Opera asked.

"The President," she said, rolling her eyes.

"Of the United States??" I squeaked.

She nodded. "Third time he's called this morning. I hate it when world powers break into tears."

"Not me, *burp*." Opera grinned. "I kinda likes it."

Wall Street turned and shoved a briefcase the size of Cleveland at me. "Here, these are for you to sign."

"What are they?"

"Endorsements, movie deals, that billion-dollar mansion you bought at the other end of town."

"A billion-dollar mansion?"

"Well, one of them, yeah." With that she turned and started back into the helicopter, just as the school bell rang.

"Where are you going?" I asked.

"Gotta negotiate that deal for you to appear on the cover of *Sports Illustrated*."

"I'm going to be on the cover of *Sports Illustrated*?"

"Not one cover, *twelve* covers. I wanted more, but there's only twelve months in a year."

I blinked, not believing my ears.

"So we'll see you later."

"But what about school?" I shouted. "You're going to miss Mr. Reptenson's science quiz. It's coming up first period."

"I dropped out of school months ago. You know that."

"You dropped out of school?!"

She buckled in as the helicopter revved up. "Of course! Somebody has to manage your career."

"But . . . dropping out of school?!" I shouted. "That's stupid! What about getting your education?"

The chopper started to rise. "Who needs an education when there's all that money to be made . . . and it's all off you."

"But . . . it's school!" I shouted. "You need an education. You need . . ."

No longer hearing me, she waved as the helicopter rose up and into the clouds.

I couldn't believe it. Wall Street had actually dropped out of school because of me? That was terrible!

Feeling sad, I turned and started toward the classrooms.

"Hey, Wally!" Opera shouted. "Where yas goin'?"

"We've got to take Reptenson's quiz."

"Yeah, right," he said, smirking.

I came to a stop. "Don't tell me you dropped out, too?"

"Nah, *burp*. But me and da boys, we don't got to take tests no more. And yas don't got to neither."

I frowned. "Why not?"

He began cracking his knuckles one after the other. "Let's just say (CRACK) dat dem teachers (CRACK, CRACK), they're all afraid (CRACK, CRACK, CRACK) of giving us bad grades (CRACK)."

My mouth dropped to the ground. "You're bullying the teachers into giving you passing grades?!"

"Nah (CRACK, CRACK, CRACK), not passing grades." Since he'd run out of fingers, he kicked off his shoes and started working on his toes. "Straight-A (CRACK) grades. *Burp!*"

\* \* \* \* \*

Soccer tryouts weren't much better.

When I got out on the field, there wasn't a soul in sight. Just a hundred trophies on the bench with a note from Coach Hurtumuch.

Dear Sir Wally,
Since you're such a great superstar, everyone on the team is embarrassed to play with you. You are now the school's entire soccer team . . . and coaching staff. Good luck!
Coach Hurtumuch

I was stunned. I couldn't believe no one wanted to play with me. What about Sophie Stompuregut? I mean, soccer meant everything to her. I glanced back down at the note.

P.S. Sophie Stompuregut is so discouraged that she's given up soccer and is now teaching coloring classes at the preschool.

I felt my throat tighten and my eyes begin to burn. Soccer had been Sophie's whole life. I just wanted to score higher than her, not destroy her.

And what about all the trophies on the bench? I looked back down at the note.

P.P.S. Since all of the schools are afraid to play you, they have also quit, which automatically makes us All State Champions. Yea team!

\* \* \* \* \*

When I finally started for home, I knew things were not good when I tried three different mansions before I found the right one.

I knew things were "notter" than not good . . . not only because Opera's grammar was wearing off on me, but because I found one of my older twin brothers, Burt (or was it Brock?), floating on a mattress in our indoor pool with five beautiful babes peeling grapes for him.

Then there was Brock (or was it Burt?) driving his gold-plated Jet Ski (it's kind of a big pool) around Burt (or was it Brock?), while pulling Mom, who was parasailing behind him (it's kind of a big room).

"Hey, Mom," I shouted. "Where's Dad?"

"Upstairs in his chair watching the game."

I let out a sigh of relief. It was good to know that at least one thing hadn't changed. I entered the nearby elevator, searched the buttons until I spotted the one labeled

DAD'S FLOOR,

and pressed it.

I shot up what seemed like twenty to thirty stories until the doors finally opened and, sure enough, there was Dad sitting in his favorite recliner watching a football game.

The only problem was, the game wasn't on TV. Instead, he sat before an entire football field that he had all to himself . . . well, except for the two pro teams playing against each other for him.

I blinked nervously. I had no idea the world's greatest soccer star could make so much money.

Don't get me wrong, I was glad to help out my family . . . but I was getting a serious feeling that things were going seriously wrong.

# Chapter 5
## Don't Forget to Floss

Things were getting more and more confusing, so I decided to work on my superhero story. It wasn't hard to find my Ol' Imax. (It used to be my Ol' Betsy, but even she had changed. And with her screen filling my entire five-story bedroom wall, what other name could I give her?)

When we last left Pudgy Boy, he'd been asked to hold off ordering his pizza so he could save the world. (Talk about a sacrifice.)

But it just might be worth it. Because everywhere he looks people are walking skin and bones...and getting skinnier and bonier by the minute.

And not just people; so are their pets...

Poodles are passing out from too many pull-ups.

Turtles are tipsy from trotting on treadmills.

Parakeets are panting from a plethora (trust me, it's a word) of push-ups.

And cats...of course, they're too lazy to do anything but sleep (except cough up an occasional fur ball).

Without a moment to spare, our plumpish pal races across the Fat Cave and hops into his Blubbermobile, only to discover

*K-Squish*

it's five sizes too small!

(I don't want to say it shrank, but picture a VW Beetle left in the clothes dryer on extra hot for forty-five minutes, give or take a month.)

Using all of his supersized hero-ics (plus a can of bacon grease that he keeps handy for just such occa-sions), our hero squirms his way out of the

*KER-Pop!*

car and races toward his Micro-Flab
computer for answers.

But even his computer is getting
skinnier (whose isn't?). Within moments,
he can no longer get his chubby fingers
on the shrinking keys.

Looking around, he sees the entire Fat
Cave downsizing in a major he-better-
get-out-before-he-becomes-its-cream-
filled-center kind of way.

He rushes to the exit and barely
squeezes through before he is met by
six skinny men with six not-so-skinny
guns.

"This is the F.B.I."

"Great!" our hero shouts.

"Waddle away from the cave with
your ham hocks up!"

"You don't understand," our hero
explains. "I'm the good guy!"

"You're under arrest."

"No, no, no! You're the Federal
Bureau of Investigation. You're supposed to help me catch the bad guys."

"Sorry, sir, we are now the Fitness
Bureau of Indigestion. And according
to our Flab-O-Meter, you've got way
too much pudge."

Quickly, our hero searches his mind. (Luckily, with so little to work with, it takes only 2.4 seconds.) In a flash of perspiration, he turns to the leader and asks:

"Say there, you look great. Have you been losing weight?"

The leader lowers his gun, blushing slightly. "Why, yes, a little—can you tell?"

"Oh, yes," our hero says, smiling. "And that bulletproof vest you're wearing is so very flattering."

"Well, thank you."

"Sir," the assistant agent calls.

Pudgy Boy turns to him. "And you. Did you know that wearing vertical stripes will make you look thinner?"

"Really?"

"Oh, yes. They could make you look at least five pounds lighter."

"Wow!"

But before they can run off to SprawlMart for a new wardrobe, a third agent shouts, "Sir, it's a trap! He's pretending to care about weight just so he can escape!"

Our husky hero spins to him and

shouts, "How can you say such a terrible thing without any proof?"

"Proof? I'll show you proof!"

Suddenly, the agent produces a giant chocolate cake (complete with double-fudge chunky-chocolate frosting) and sets it on the ground in front of our hero.

Pudgy Boy looks at it and begins to sweat.

Then he begins to shake.

Soon he drops to his knees, drooling like Homer Simpson over a box of doughnuts.

"So you like it, do you?" the agent taunts.

"Does it come with fries?" our hero asks.

"Regular or supersize?"

Sensing a trap, Pudgy Boy uses all of his superhero strength to resist. But it does no good! Before he can help himself, he shouts: "SUPERSIZE ME!"

Suddenly, the truth becomes clear, and the agents swarm in.

Suddenlier, our hero is handcuffed and thrown into the fatty wagon.

"Where am I going!?" he shouts.

"To the Fat Farm," the agent yells. "That's where you will be taught to hate yourself for being overweight."

"But I like myself!"

"Don't worry, we'll take care of that!"

Within minutes, the fatty wagon rolls through the gates of Alkaflab Prison, where our polysaturated pal is escorted past all sorts of prisoners undergoing rehabilitation.

Here he sees:

—Girls forced to stare at photos of models with skimpy bodies wearing microskimpy clothes.

—Boys taunted for belonging to the chess club instead of the lettermen's club.

—Grownups being sold memberships to gyms they will never go to after the first week.

Great beanpoles! Who will rescue our hero before it's too late?

More important, whatever happened to our bad guy, Boney Boy?

And most important, did they just leave that chocolate cake on the ground at the Fat Cave so nobody gets to eat it?

These and weightier worries weigh upon our overweight wonder, when suddenly—

"Hey there," a familiar voice said. "How'd it go?"

I glanced around, trying to find out where the voice came from. It sounded so close, but there wasn't a horse in sight.

"Where are you?" I asked.

"In here."

"Where?"

"Your mouth."

"My mouth!"

"Don't shout, I'm right here."

"But—" I swallowed nervously.

"Don't do that either!!"

I stopped swallowing and settled for a nervous breath.

"Thanks, that's a lot better."

I stuck out my tongue but couldn't see a thing. "Wha ar ou oing in ma mouf?" I asked.

"I'm tooth plaque."

"Ooth aque!?"

"Yeah, something like that. You know, those little germ thingies that sit on your teeth ready to make cavities."

"Wealwy?"

"Really. By the way, thanks for not brushing tonight. It's going to make my job a lot easier."

I pulled in my tongue but was afraid to close my lips. "Wha appen oo da horss?"

"Got me—it's your imagination, not mine. So how's it going?"

"Nat so ood."

"Now, there's a surprise. So what do you want to do?"

"I wan to go all da way."

"All the way?"

"Yeah, I wan to go po."

"You want to go pro?"

I nodded. "Tings ar too weird eing in school."

"So you think going totally pro is the answer?"

It was getting tougher and tougher not to swallow, so I just shrugged.

"What about the other kids?"

"It ill ee etter."

"You think so?"

I wanted to explain how getting Opera away from school would be better for him (and all his little victims). And how, if I wasn't around, poor

Sophie could actually play on the team again. Come to think of it, we'd actually have a team.

I wanted to say all those things, but I was so worried about not swallowing that I just nodded.

"What about your family?"

"Wha abou em?"

"You think giving them all this money and letting them have whatever they want whenever they want it is a good thing?"

"Sluur." (It was supposed to be "sure," but right now my tongue was drowning in saliva.) "En fak, F wan oo iv em ore."

"Well, all right then. Starting at midnight, your family will have unlimited funds and you'll be playing with the big boys. No kid stuff. No school. You'll be totally pro."

I wasn't crazy about no school, but I guess a guy's gotta make some sacrifices. So I nodded and gave him a thumbs-up.

"An I swallow ow?" I asked.

"As soon as you wake up, sure."

"Ake up?"

"Even the great Wally McDoogle couldn't dream up something this weird without, you know, *dreaming* it up."

I nodded again. It made as much sense as anything else.

"Here, let me help."

"Elp?"

"Yeah." He took a deep breath (Does plaque breathe? Who knows; who cares?) and shouted:

# "WAKE UP!"

My head shot up as my eyes popped open.

And, sure enough, I was back in my fancy bedroom staring at my five-story screen with the Pudgy Boy story on it. Not a thing had changed. Well, except for the lake of saliva growing in my mouth. The lake of saliva I immediately

*Gulp, Gulp, Gulp*ed

down (yum) as I headed for the bathroom.

I wasn't sure if what really happened had, you know, really happened. But one thing was sure. I was definitely going to brush, and even floss, before I went back to sleep.

# Chapter 6

## Perfection! ... and other impossible dreams

I have to tell you, it felt great to finally have created the perfect reality.

Now, at last, I would have everything I ever wanted.

Now, at last, I could use all my talents and skills.

Now, at last, things would really begin unraveling and getting weirder and weirderer . . .

First, there was Burt (or was it Brock?).

I suspected there might be a problem when I got to the breakfast table (which was now solid gold and thirty feet long) and saw my brother at the other end. That wasn't the problem (though seeing my brother when he's just gotten up is always a scary thing). The problem was, he was lying in a hospital bed!

"Burt (or is it Brock?)!" I shouted as I raced to his side. "What's wrong?"

He moved his lips, but his voice was too faint to hear. Fortunately, one of his two dozen nurses translated:

"He wants you to get someone to breathe for him."

"What are you talking about?!" I cried.

"You've given him everything he's ever wanted. Now he wants you to get someone to breathe for him."

"That's crazy!" I said, shaking my head. "And why is he in that bed? What's wrong with him?"

The nurse answered, "You've hired so many servants to do things for him that his muscles have withered away to nothing."

"You mean he can't walk?"

"Or sit or talk or eat or drink."

"He couldn't have gotten that lazy!"

"Sure he could; after all, we're talking about your brother Brock (or is it Burt?)."

I noticed another nurse sitting beside him eating piles of bacon, ham, sausage, scrambled eggs, fried eggs, poached eggs, hash browns, hot cakes, waffles, and a giant stack of toast with strawberry jelly.

"What's she doing?" I demanded.

"Eating his food," the nurse explained.

"You don't mean . . . ?"

"That's right," she said, nodding, "your brother's too lazy to chew it."

Suddenly, a gross thought ran through my mind. "What about the swallowing?" I asked. "Who does the swallowing?!"

*(I told you it was gross.)*

"Relax," the nurse assured me. "She does."

"Because . . . ?"

"Because he's too lazy to even swallow it."

I felt a slight wave of relief. But only slight. "And my other brother? Where is he?"

"Prison," the nurse answered.

"Prison?!"

"He wanted some baby's lollipop, and you wouldn't buy it for him, so he stole it."

"He's in prison for stealing a lollipop?!"

"No, he's in prison for stealing the baby who wouldn't let go of the lollipop."

I turned from the table, my head spinning faster than our cat the time she got caught in the dryer. Using all of my strength, I cried out to the one person who could fix any mess ever made. I mean, you name it, and she'd cleaned it.

"MOM!"

"She's not here, either," the nurse said.

"Where is she?"

"Switzerland."

"Switzerland?!"

"Yes. She was tired of cleaning up after everybody, so you bought her that nice chalet in the Swiss Alps."

"What about Dad?" I yelled. "What did Dad do when he heard she left?"

"Actually, he's never heard that she's gone. Or seen that she's gone."

I swallowed nervously. "Because . . . ?"

The nurse shrugged. "How can you see or hear anything if you've had miniature TV sets attached to your glasses and earphones implanted in your ears?"

My mouth dropped open.

"Don't look so shocked. How else could he make sure he never missed a football game?"

"And I paid for it?"

"Sure. Since he never has to go to work, you had to do something to help him fill his time."

Things were not going well. I glanced around the room. "And my little sister, Carrie? Where's she?"

"You helped Carrie start her own chain of restaurants."

My face brightened. "I did?"

"Yup. Of course, she's gone twenty billion dollars in debt because of all those food poisoning lawsuits. But at least she's got a catchy slogan."

"Which is?" I asked, expecting the worst.

The nurse cleared her throat and recited:

Enjoy your food twice as much—
once going down, Once coming up!

I nodded, for once not surprised.
What did surprise me was the familiar

*Whop-Whop-Whop-Whop*

of Wall Street's helicopter.

Well, I thought it was her helicopter. But when I caught the elevator and headed up to the roof, I was surprised to see that my chauffeur was the pilot.

"Hurry, Mr. McDoogle, or you'll be late for your endorsements!" he shouted.

"Where's Wall Street?" I yelled as I stepped inside and moved past the same tennis court, home theater, and hot tub as my limo. (I guess some things never change.)

"Where's *who*?" the chauffeur shouted back to me.

"My best friend, Wall Street!"

"You mean President Wall Street?"

"President?" I shouted as we lifted off from the roof.

"Yes. She's still your sports manager, but

she's made so much money off you that she was
also able to buy the entire country—well, except
for California, which of course isn't really part
of the country."

"Wall Street is President?" I shouted. "That's
great!"

"Yes, sir. Well, except for all the riots and
demonstrations."

"Riots and demonstrations?"

"Some folks aren't crazy about all the new
taxes she's created."

"Taxes? Why did she create taxes?"

"How else can she become the richest person
on the planet?"

"What types of taxes?" I shouted.

"Well, let's see, there's the one she's added
for skateboarding."

"A skateboarding tax? You're kidding!"

"And the one on dodge ball."

"A dodge ball tax?!"

"And don't even ask about the speech tax."

"Speech tax? But this is the United States of
America! We have free speech!"

"Actually, it's now the United States of Wall
Street. And speech is free only if you've got the
money to buy it."

"Money?!"

"Fifty cents a word—except for those fancy-schmancy ones they use on TV news shows. They cost seventy-five cents."

I sat back in my seat, stunned. I knew Wall Street could get a bit greedy, but this . . .

Reaching for the remote, I flipped on the TV and came face-to-screen with another surprise. There, in all of his yelling glory, was my other best friend . . . Opera.

Only, instead of going around bullying little kids all day at school, he was standing on some wrestling-ring ropes and screaming:

"I WILL, *burp,* DESTROY YOU!
I WILL, *burp,* ANNIHILATE YOU!
I WILL, *burp,* TERMINATE YOU!"

(And that was just his greeting to a visiting kindergarten class—
don't even ask what he was yelling at his opponent.)

I have to admit it was a little hard recognizing him with the black hood over his face and the additional five thousand pounds of fat he'd gained. Of course, the giant skull and crossbones tattooed across his back didn't help much, either.

But there was no missing the headphones attached to his ears, the Chippy Chipper potato-chip crumbs falling from his pierced lips, and, of course, his ever-present *burping*!

By the looks of things, Opera had taken the art of bullying to a brand-new depth.

The fact that he was jumping off the ropes and crushing some grandmother in a wheelchair who'd just booed him made the depth even deeper.

I shouted to the chauffeur, "So Opera is a professional wrestler?"

"Yes, sir. He got so good at destroying fans trying to talk to you that he decided to make a full-time living at destroying other folks."

I shook my head. Hard to believe that so few changes could make things go so bad.

But, as you might have already guessed, the badness had barely begun . . .

\* \* \* \* \*

Ten minutes later, my helicopter set down in a TV studio parking lot. And there, among the million fans waiting to greet me, was my old buddy.

"Wall Street!" I shouted.

I hopped out of the chopper and raced for her. But I'd barely taken a step before a dozen Secret Service agents

*K-Thud*—"OAFF!"

tackled me to the ground and immediately started to strip-search

*Rip*—"OW!"
*Tear*—"OUCH!"
*Shred, Shred, Shred*—"STOP THAT!"

me.

Actually, it wasn't that big of a problem until they completed their search and left me standing ⅞ naked before my millions of adoring fans.

(Now you know why they call it a "strip search.")

Fortunately, the remaining ⅛ of my clothes included my underwear—well, at least the important parts.

Unfortunately, there was still enough of my body showing to make my fans go nuts. What can I say? Pretty soon, everyone was screaming hysterically:

*"AWWK!* PUT SOME CLOTHES ON!"
*"EEK!* IT SHOULD BE ILLEGAL
TO LOOK LIKE THAT!"
*"ARRK!* I THINK I'M GOING TO—
(BLaaaaa . . . )
—NEVER MIND, IT'S TOO LATE!"

Wall Street arrived at my side and helped me toward the studio. "Sorry about that," she said. "But I've made lots of enemies, and we can't be too careful."

I nodded, resetting my neck and checking other items in need of repair.

We entered the hallway, and I was immediately met by the director. He was throwing up his hands and doing what directors do best—screaming instructions at a bunch of people.

"HURRY, HURRY, HURRY! WE'RE TAPING HIS ENDORSEMENT IN FIVE MINUTES!"

Suddenly, a bunch of makeup and wardrobe folks swarmed all over me.

"What am I endorsing?" I called to Wall Street.

She said something, but I couldn't hear over all the screaming.

"FOUR MINUTES, PEOPLE. FOUR MINUTES!"

Moments later, I was standing in front of a bunch of cameras wearing more makeup than an entire goth band and so much eyeliner even Michael Jackson would be jealous.

"STAND BY, PEOPLE!" the director screamed. "STAND BY!"

I spotted Wall Street by one of the cameras and again asked, "What am I endorsing?"

"Just read the cue cards," she said.

"But—"

"Trust me."

Coming from Wall Street, those were not exactly the words I wanted to hear.

A guy with one of those clapper board thingies leaped in front of my face and shouted: "World hunger commercial, take one!" He clapped it shut and disappeared.

I turned to Wall Street and whispered hopefully, "World hunger? We're doing a promo about world hunger?"

"That's right," she said, smiling. "We're doing a commercial about world hunger."

I smiled back. I can't tell you how relieved I was to hear that she was finally using her power for someone other than herself.

"AND . . . ACTION!" the director screamed.

I turned toward the cameras, looked at the cue card, and began to read:

**"HI THERE. AS YOU ALL KNOW, I'M WALLY MCDOOGLE, THE WORLD-FAMOUS SOCCER PLAYER."**

Even as I said the lines, I kept thinking how things were finally working out. Sure, I had my worries at the beginning, but now it looked like everything was turning around.

"AND AS SOMEONE SO INCREDIBLY
SUCCESSFUL, I CAN'T TELL YOU HOW
STRONGLY I ENDORSE WORLD HUNGER."

I frowned slightly. That didn't quite make
sense, but I kept on reading:

"THAT'S WHY I'M EXCITED ABOUT THESE
FABULOUS NEW NUTRITION BARS, *Eat All
You Want.*"

I held up the bar one of the props people had
slipped into my hand.

"WHY, WITH JUST THREE BARS A DAY,
YOU'LL NEVER GET FULL AGAIN.
YOU'LL BE ABLE TO EAT ALL DAY LONG
WITHOUT EVER HAVING TO STOP."

I glanced at Wall Street with a look of con-
cern, but she kept motioning me to read—

"AND IF YOU'RE ALWAYS EATING ALL THE
TIME . . . YOU, TOO, CAN DO YOUR PART
TO SUPPORT WORLD HUNGER. YOU, TOO,
CAN MAKE SURE THERE WILL *NEVER* BE
ENOUGH FOOD, SO OTHERS WILL *ALWAYS*
BE STARVING TO—"

"Hold it; wait a minute," I said. "That's not right."

"CUT, CUT, CUT!" the director screamed.

I headed over to Wall Street and did my own version of getting angry. "You lied to me! You said I'd be promoting the cause of world hunger!"

"That's exactly what you're doing," she said. "You're promoting world hunger so we'll always have it."

"That's terrible!"

"How can it be terrible if it's making me even more money?"

"This is nuts!" I shoved the *EAT ALL YOU WANT* bar into her hands. "You're making money off other people's suffering!"

"Not if you don't do your part. Now, get in there and promote these puppies!" She shoved the bar back into my hands.

I couldn't believe my ears. "No way!" I shouted. "This is crazy!" I turned to storm off.

Unfortunately, all those Secret Service agents had other ideas. They suddenly formed a human wall around me.

I twirled back to Wall Street. "Are you saying I can't leave?"

She shrugged. "You can leave anytime you want . . . just as long as you finish the commercial."

I stood there blinking. Had she really turned into such a monster? "Are you serious?" I demanded. "You actually expect me to do this commercial?"

She nodded. "And the other."

"The other??"

"Sure, we still have to sell my new *Three-in-One Health Shots*."

*"Three-in-One Health Shots?"*

"That's right." She grinned. "One shot and you'll get three sicknesses—measles, mumps, and malaria."

I couldn't believe my ears. "But . . . *why*?!" I demanded.

She looked at me as if I were the crazy one. "Because if people don't have the disease, how can I sell them the cure?"

I could only stare. Wall Street was no longer just making money off my misfortunes . . . now she was making it off everybody's.

"So let's get started," she said, grinning again. "The sooner we finish these endorsements, the sooner we can get to the stadium and start that game."

The game. I closed my eyes, afraid to even imagine what that would be like.

# Chapter 7

## Let the Game Begin!

I got to the stadium just in time to suit up and run onto the field with my incredibly professional team.

The good news was, I was still the world's greatest soccer player.

The bad news was, I still had my seventh-grade body, which, as you may recall, isn't always the strongest (or most pain-resistant).

My first problem came when my fellow players slapped me on the back:

"Okay, Wally!" *(K-Bamb)*

"Here we go, Wally!" *(K-Slap)*

"Let's do it, Wally!" *(K-Slam)*

These, of course, were followed by the usual reactions of my falling face-first *(K-Splat!)*

*K-Smash! K-Smooch!*

onto the field and being run over by other players.

But it wasn't that bad. After eating the daily minimum requirement of turf (at least I was getting enough greens in my diet), I was ready to go.

We got the ball at the kickoff and headed downfield.

One of the halfbacks passed it to me, and I must say I was brilliant.

I did everything . . . I dribbled, I faked, I headed, I bicycle-kicked. And after four or five minutes of these amazing feats, one of my teammates had an even more amazing idea:

"Hey, Wally, why not try moving it downfield!"

I told you these guys were pros!

And so I got the chance to do it all over again—kicking, dribbling, faking.

Finally, I got into the box and tried something even more exciting . . . getting slide-tackled, getting face-elbowed, and getting body-

*K-SLAMM*ed

onto the ground.

Now, I don't want to say the other team played dirty, but I kept asking myself why their uniforms were striped with prison inmate numbers stenciled on the back.

(And don't even ask about all the watchdogs and jail guards surrounding the field.)

"Who are those guys?" I groaned as they dumped whatever pieces of my body they could find onto a stretcher.

"They're the Penitentiary Players," the team doctor answered.

"They're from a prison?!" I cried.

"Don't be silly."

I relaxed ever so slightly.

"They're from lots of prisons."

I tensed ever so muchly. "WHAT?!"

"It was your manager's idea," the doctor said as they carried me to the sidelines. "People are paying tons of money to see death-row inmates play you in soccer."

The good news was, the doctor had me back on my feet and in the game in no time.

The bad news was, the doctor had me back on my feet and in the game in no time.

"Are you really sure I'm ready?" I shouted over my shoulder. "I mean, really, really, really, really sure?"

"Don't worry," he yelled back. "We've put calls into organ-transplant banks across the country. They'll have replacements waiting for you just as soon as you finish the game."

Little did he know the game was about to finish me.

"Wally," a teammate shouted, "heads up!"

I spun around just in time to see the ball coming at me. It was a perfect setup for a header. The goalie was out of position and there was no defense around me—well, except for one mountain of muscle flying at me sideways with his cleats pointed straight at my chest. Steel cleats which, I might point out, had been filed to some very sharp and very long tips.

Very sharp and very long steel tips that looked like they were about to perform some very deep and painful open-heart surgery.

Being a little short on medical insurance, and being the incredible superstar that I am, I did what any incredible superstar short on medical insurance would do:

I dropped to my knees and screamed:

# "MOMMY!"

Of course, Mommy was still in Switzerland.

And the big bruiser with the killer cleats?

Well, the good news was, those cleats never found me.

The bad news was, all 372 pounds of Bruiser's personal prisoner poundage

*K-WHAM!*
*stagger-stagger-stagger*

(Gee, I think now would be a good time
to pass out for a day or two.)

### *K-THUD*

did.

\* \* \* \* \*

"So how's it going, *sniff*?"

Though he was all stuffy-sounding, I didn't even have to open my eyes to recognize the voice.

"Not so good," I groaned.

"Hmm, I wonder why, *cough-cough*. Oh, ledt me guess, maybe because God knows whadt He's doing after all?"

(I just hate smart-alecky overactive imaginations, don't you?)

Finally, I pried open my eyes and saw . . . nothing. No bright lights, no horses, and, as far as I could tell, no tooth plaque.

"Where are you?" I asked. "What are you this time?"

"I'm your house."

"My house? Houses can't talk!"

"Righdt, and like horses and tooth plaque, *sniff*, can?"

"Do you have a cold?"

"Not a coldt, but—a-h-h-choo!—allergies."

"What's a house doing with allergies?"

"Wally, if you were a house, where wouldt your head be?"

"I don't know . . . in the attic, I guess."

"Very goodt. And have you seen how much, *cough-cough*, dust is in your attic?"

I slowly nodded, getting his point.

"So," he asked, "are you finally learning thadt God knows whadt's best? Thadt there's a reason for everything He does?"

Now, the way I figured it, I had two choices. Admit I was wrong, or figure out a way to fix the few problems that had come up and—

"Few problems?!" the voice interrupted.

"I didn't say that."

"You thoughdt it, *sniff*."

"Who said you could read my mind?"

"Who saidt overactive imaginations can'dt?"

(I just hate know-it-all overactive imaginations, don't you?)

"I heardt that!"

"All right, all right," I said. "I'll admit things aren't running too smoothly. I had no idea all that money would make my family nuts."

"Or all that power wouldt ruin Wall Streedt . . . or all that fame wouldt ruin Opera . . . or—"

"All right, all right," I said, scrunching up my brows. "Just let me think a little."

"Uh-oh, now we're in, *sniff*, dtrouble."

"Shh!"

"Who you telling dto shh, *cough-cough*? Why, without me you wouldn't have any superhero stories. Facdt is, you wouldn't even be writing these weird books, which, I mighdt poindt oudt, are getting weirder and weird—"

"If you don't be quiet, I'll imagine you don't exist."

"Whadt??"

"You heard me."

"You can'dt use your imagination to imagine your imagination dtoesn't exisdt."

"Says who?"

The house grew strangely quiet, except for some stuffy wheezing. Apparently, I'd made my point. I continued to think, slowly forming a plan.

"You know," I said, "all those things that have happened would still be okay, if . . ."

"If whadt?"

"If there was no way for people to get hurt."

"Come, *wheeze-cough*, again?"

"If there was no way for people to get hurt, Wall Street could still have all that power, Opera could still have all that fame—"

"And you'dt still be on that soccer field playing."

"Exactly," I said. "So what do you think?"

"I think that last dtackle did you some serious brain damage."

I ignored him. I'd made my decision. "So that's what I want," I said.

"Whadt?"

"No pain."

"For you?"

"For everyone. Starting midnight tonight, no one in the entire world will ever feel pain again."

"Are you, *cough-wheeze*, sure?"

"Sure, I'm sure."

"Oh, brother . . ." He sighed.

"What does that mean?"

"Idt means buckle in, 'cause you ain'dt seen nothin'

# AHH-CHOO!

yedt . . ."

The sneeze woke me up, and I turned over on my side to look at the alarm clock. It read:

## 11:32

I had half an hour before the changes would go into effect. And so, with nothing else to do, I reached for Ol' Imax, stared at the giant screen in front of me, and got back to work on the superhero story.

# Chapter 8

## No Pain, No Brain . . .

When we last left our hefty, hunky chunk of a hero, Pudgy Boy was being thrown into the prison for the perpetual puffy.

Here he is put on a strict diet of water and water—which isn't so bad when you consider the various methods that it can be prepared. I mean, there's fried water, barbecued water, water tartare, and his favorite...a thick slab of broiled water smothered in creamy, luscious, melt-in-your-mouth, you-guessed-it, water.

Unfortunately, there is no dessert (after all, he is on a diet). But since the calorie-counting cop/chief likes him, he lets him lick the back of a postage stamp.

Yum!

The rest of the time he's being forced to buy workout DVDs that he will never watch, stylish workout clothes that he will never wear, and listen to motivational tapes telling him if he doesn't look like a toothpick, then he has no business being alive.

But where have things gone so terribly wrong?

What sort of secret beam is Boney Boy broadcasting into everyone's brain to convince them that the tiniest fraction of flab means the most major of failures? Granted, people should watch what they eat and everyone should exercise, but what has made everyone so nuts?

These are the humble thoughts haunting our hero's head as he hunkers in his cell gnawing on what's left of his mattress. (Hey, even dieters need their fiber.)

Then suddenly, out of the blue, he hears:

"Are you really giving up so easily, Pudgy Boy?"

Our hero's head snaps up, and he looks at his TV screen to see...

*Ta-da-DAAAAA!*

(After all these books,

don't make me tell you what this is.)

Could it be? Yes, it is he! It is the one, it is the only...

*Ta-da-DAAAAA!*

(Well, okay, but just for the newbies...

it's bad-guy music, all right?)

"Boney Boy," our hero gasps, "what are you doing there?"

"I've always been here, you overweight offender of all that is evil. How else do you think I'm controlling the world?"

"You're doing this to the world through TV? That's your secret weapon?"

"Of course. By controlling all the TV shows and making all the actors and actresses look like human x-rays, I can convince the rest of the world to feel like fabulously flabby failures."

"Oh, no."

"Oh, yes. And if you don't hurry up and do something, this will be the first superhero story where the superhero becomes a superfailure. But then again, since you're overweight, you probably already are."

"Already are what?"

"A failure."

And that, dear reader, is all the motivation Pudgy Boy needed.

In a flash, he's on his feet, racing to his jailhouse window.

In a flashier flash, he's whistling out a secret code.

In a flashier flash than that last flash, his Blubbermobile races around the corner and

*SCREECHes*

to a complete stop outside his prison cell....

Well, not a complete stop. There is still that lingering

*jiggle-jiggle-jiggle*

of the car's body....(Why else would they call it a Blubbermobile?)

Finally, the trunk pops open. A giant hook with an attached rope shoots out and grabs the bars of the window. (It's a good thing he paid extra money for that "100,000 Miles or One Jail Breakout" warranty.)

He gives another whistle. The Blubbermobile drops into first gear and races forward, laying a patch of

*SQUEEEAL*

rubber while taking a sizable portion of the

*CREAKKK*
*K-Rash*
*krumple, krumple, krumple*

jailhouse wall with it.

After stopping by the prison post office for an extra roll of stamps (he's in the mood for some munchies), he races to the Blubbermobile and easily slips in. (Proof that the water diet works.)

He hits the Bad-Guy Tracking Button (sold at Good-Guy Stores everywhere), and it immediately starts

*Beep-beep-beep-beep*

tracking the signal to Boney Boy's secret TV station.

Immediatelier than that last immediately, it shows the location of the secret hideout, which is...(sorry, I can't tell you, it's a secret).

But Pudgy Boy knows and that's all that counts.

Having finished off the stamps, our hero drops by the nearest $6/10\frac{1}{2}$ (it's a low-budget story, I can't afford 7/11) and grabs a dozen candy bars, a jar of pickles, a pack of sugar doughnuts, and, of course, a diet soda.

Then, quicker than you can say, "Well, what do you know, we're finally going to have a showdown between the good guy and the bad guy," our hero lets out a hearty

### *BURP!*
(must have been those pickles)

Now, fueled by more calories than a human being ought to eat in a life-time (or two), he races for Boney Boy's lair.

Who knows what dangerously diabol-ical diet our dastardly dude will dish out next?

Who knows if our hero will ever learn the importance of eating a well-balanced meal?

And, most important, can you really barbecue water?

These and other mindless messages march through his marvelously mindless mind when—

Suddenly, I looked up from Ol' Imax's keyboard. Was it possible? My entire body had stopped hurting, just like that.

Amazing. I felt absolutely no pain from the afternoon's game (or any of my other mishaps). How weird!

I reached out and lightly banged my hand on the nightstand.

Nothing.

Cool.

I banged it harder.

Still nothing.

Cooler yet.

I glanced at my clock and saw the reason. It now read:

## 12:01

All right!

I settled comfortably back into bed. Imagine, I'd just created a world with no pain. I mean, no offense, but why had God invented such a terrible thing in the first place?

It didn't matter. The point was, I'd fixed it.

Unfortunately, in just a few hours I was about to discover what a fix my fix had put us in.

\* \* \* \* \*

I woke up the next morning to hear a strange

*ZZZZZZZZT . . . ZZZZZZZZT . . .*

sound.

Leaping from my bed, I staggered into the hall to see Carrie on her hands and knees, crying.

"What's going on?" I asked.

"It's Collision," she sobbed. "She keeps sticking her nose into the electrical outlet."

I looked past her to see our family cat. Her fur was smoking and her eyes were dazed, but she just kept on

*ZZZZZZZZT . . . ZZZZZZZZT . . .*

electrocuting herself.

"It makes no sense!" Carrie cried. "It's like she can't feel the pain so she doesn't know to stop."

But, of course, it made perfect sense . . . at least to me. I had created a world without pain. And since pain could no longer warn Collision, it would soon be a world without

*ZZZZZZZZT . . . ZZZZZZZZT . . .*

Collision.

"Make her stop, Wally!" Carrie pleaded. "Please, before she kills herself!"

Only then did I realize that I might have made a minor mistake. There might actually be a reason to feel pain. At least in our kitty's case.

Unfortunately, there were a few other cases as well.

Like when I was flying to the soccer stadium for our game.

It was the weirdest thing, but when I looked out of the helicopter window, I saw the cars below purposely

*SCREEECH . . .*
*K-rash*ing

into one another.

"What's going on down there?" I shouted to the pilot.

"Just your morning traffic jam."

"But they keep smashing into each other!"

"Yeah, it makes it more interesting."

"Interesting??" I shouted. "What about getting hurt?"

*"Hurt?"* he asked.

"Yeah, what about all the pain?"

"There is no pain," he called back.

I looked out the window, and sure enough, he was right. People were dragging themselves out of their cars with broken arms, broken legs, and your general, all-around broken bodies. But instead of rushing to the hospital for help, they just stood around pointing and shouting at one another.

"Somebody has to do something!" I yelled.

"Why?"

"Everybody's getting hurt!"

"I told you, nobody gets hurt," he shouted back.

"They don't feel any of that?!"

"Not a thing."

"But they could be dying!"

"Yeah." He shrugged. "Sometimes it happens, we're not sure why."

But I was sure. Just like with Collision, pain had a purpose. It was to warn us that we'd hurt ourselves; it was an alarm telling us to go get fixed.

I couldn't stand to watch anymore. The scene below was just too awful. So I reached for the TV remote and surfed channels until I found a wrestling match. Sure enough, there was my old buddy, Opera. Maybe watching him would take my mind off all the junk that was happening below.

Unfortunately, things were no better with him.

Instead of jumping on little old ladies, he was jumping on everybody!

That's right, people were standing in line begging for him to jump on them. And he did. One

*K-SMASH!*

after another

*K-SMASH!*

after another.

It was terrible. Worse than the traffic accidents. Because instead of just pulverizing the spectators (who crawled out from under him laughing and bleeding), he was also pulverizing himself.

With every fall, he'd smash or break something in his own body. In minutes, he looked like some grotesque monster with broken bones sticking out every which way.

But he didn't seem to care.

And the reason was simple. Like everybody else in the world, he no longer felt pain.

I closed my eyes, afraid I'd seen it all. But, of course, I hadn't. There was still the soccer match . . .

The good news was, we were no longer playing that all-star team of prisoners.

The bad news was, we were no longer feeling any pain.

Most of all me . . .

I'll save you the gory details (well, most of them anyway). Let's just say it was a close game and I was my usual brilliant self. Of course, there were a few ruined body parts here and there, but it didn't matter. After all, since I felt no pain I just kept playing and playing . . . and playing some more.

It didn't matter that by the third period both of my ankles were broken (which was okay, except for the part of my feet pointing backward). It didn't matter that I had to use both of my hands to hold my head onto my shoulders. (Who uses hands in soccer, anyway?) What mattered was the score was 3 to 3, and we were coming down to the last 20 seconds of play.

That's when I snagged the ball from a corner kick. And, as the sweeper, I started up the field, going coast to coast, outmaneuvering every opponent that came my way.

(The fact that my feet pointed backward seemed to confuse them a bit.)

We were down to 15 seconds by the time I reached midfield.

The crowd was on their feet, shouting:

"Wall-y! Wall-y! Wall-y!"

10 seconds.

There was no doubt about it, I was going all the way.

5 seconds.

It was now or never. I leaned back, preparing to deliver a sensational kick, when I suddenly received a sensational

*K-STOMP!*

by a 372-pound defender (with some very familiar, sharp steel cleats).

I would have loved to ask him if he had a twin brother serving time in prison, but it's hard to ask anything when you've been stomped flatter than a pancake that's been smashed by a dump truck that's been rolled over by a steam-roller.

And yet, since I felt no pain, I hadn't lost con-sciousness. This meant I could go for the penalty kick and possibly score the winning point.

All right, what luck!

Of course, I would have been more lucky if my paper-thin body wasn't flapping around like a Fourth of July flag in a Fourth of July hurri-cane. (You try being smashed by a dump truck that's been rolled over by a steamroller and tell me what you look like.)

Unfortunately, as soon as the ref blew the whistle . . . I blew over.

Un-unfortunately (which I guess is the same as fortunately), I was immediately hit by a pow-erful gust of wind.

Suddenly, my paper-thin leg flapped harder than Collision's back leg when she's digging for fleas.

Suddenlier, I kicked the ball, sending it fly-ing toward the goal.

Suddenliest, the goalie (who'd been rolling on the ground laughing at my flag-flapping rou-tine) let the ball get by and score the winning point!

The crowd went nuts, chanting their usual:

"Wall-y! Wall-y! Wall-y!"

as my team members scraped me off the grass and carried me on their shoulders.

Yes sir, life could not have been better. Once again, I was a star—though a stupendously stomped one.

But even as they carried me toward the locker room, clinging to my legs so I wouldn't blow away, I knew things still weren't right. I knew I still had to make one last change.

One that would prevent 372-pound bruisers from flattening soccer stars.

One that would prevent Opera from splatting himself on wrestling fans.

One that would prevent drivers from destroying themselves.

Little did I know it would also prevent the country, in fact, the entire earth, from surviving.

# Chapter 9

## Up, Up, and Away

"No gravity!" cried the talking air freshener (who sounded a lot like my overactive imagination). "Are you crazy?!"

"No, listen," I argued. "Without gravity people will no longer get hurt by falling down."

"You mean you'll no longer get stomped by overweight soccer players."

"And Opera will never get hurt because he'll just float over those wrestling fans, and cars will never crash because they'll just float over each other. I mean, think of all the problems it will solve."

"I'm thinking of all the problems you've started. Why don't you just admit that God's ways are the best and—"

"No, no, no, this will work. I promise you, this will work."

"All right, then." He gave a heavy sigh (which

smelled a lot like cinnamon-clove-lilac spray). "Starting at midnight there will be no gravity."

Yes sir, that was pretty much the way I remembered the conversation that night.

And that was pretty much the reality I woke up to the following morning.

\* \* \* \* \*

For starters, it was fantastic. I mean, just lifting off the covers and floating out of bed was incredible . . .

No cold floors for your bare feet to walk on.

No hallway toys for you to fall over.

And no good way to spit after brushing your teeth.

(Well, all right, but two out of three's not so bad. Er, two out of four if you count trying to use the toilet.)

Unfortunately, things got a little worse when I floated downstairs to see . . .

"WALLY, *glug, glug,* HELP, *glug, glug,* us!"

It was Burt (or was it Brock—whichever one was on leave from the hospital—or was it prison?). It didn't matter. Like everyone else in my family, he was busy drowning in a giant blob of water that floated in our mansion's living room!

"What happened?!" I shouted.

"It's Brock's (or is it Burt's?) swimming pool!" Carrie shouted. "All the water has floated up and out of it!"

"And not just the pool!" Dad shouted as he pointed at the news on his eyeglass TV screens, which were busy

*K-SNAPP*ing, *K-RACK*ing, and
*K-SHORT*ing

out from the water. "All of the lakes and even the oceans are floating up and away from their shores!"

Before I could answer, even more water began pouring in. This time from an open door. Apparently a nearby river had also floated out of its banks!

But it wasn't just water pouring in. There were also:

—people no longer able to walk on the
  sidewalks,
—cars no longer able to drive on the roads,
—skateboarders no longer able to race
  illegally through shopping malls.

Everything that had rested on the ground was now floating (including the kitty litter from

*cough-cough, gag-gag, spit-spit*
"Gross!"

Collision's cat box!).

Everywhere people were crashing into things . . . and getting crashed into by things. But since there was no pain, it didn't matter. They just kept crashing and crashing and crashing until they started dying and dying and dying!

Suddenly, what had been a dream had turned into a nightmare!

The phone that drifted by started to ring. I reached up and answered, "Hello!"

"Wally!"

"Wall Street?!" I shouted. "Where are you?"

"I'm on Air Force One, flying into outer space."

"Outer space?!"

"There's no gravity to hold my plane down, so we're flying out-of-control into the cosmos."

"That's terrible!"

"No, it's deadly! I only have a few minutes of oxygen left before I die!"

"Oh, no!" I said.

"Oh, yes!" she said. "And poor Opera, he's already gone!"

"*Gone?*"

"With all that burping, he propelled himself

past the moon. And since he didn't have any oxygen—"

"You mean . . ." I swallowed. "Opera's dead?!"

"Hey, he got off lucky. At least he had a great view. But everyone else will be dying from sheer panic and mayhem."

"This is terrible!" I cried. "What do I do?!"

"You're the one with the overactive imagination. I thought you'd know."

Desperately, I looked at the chaos surrounding me—just as a surfer floated out of the kitchen, barely missing my head with his board.

"Listen," Wall Street continued, "I'd love to chat, but I've only got a few more minutes of air. And with all the bad junk I've done, I figure I better use the rest of my time praying."

"But—"

"See ya, Wally. And thanks for everything!" Then, just like that, the phone went dead.

I had to do something! Things were getting worse by the second!

Turning around, I ducked past a rhinoceros floating by (apparently there was no gravity at the zoo, either) and drifted back up the stairs to my room.

Once there, I shut the door and shouted, "Overactive Imagination?!"

There was no answer.

"OVERACTIVE IMAGINATION?!"

Still nothing. Only when the alarm clock floated by, *K-thunk*ing me on the head, did I remember why.

It was 8:30 in the morning! I had to wait a whole day until it turned midnight before I could change things!

But that was too long! By then, everyone would be—

Suddenly, the entire house

# *K-SHUDDERed.*

I floated toward the window and looked out to see that a giant iceberg had hit the house.

No, wait a minute. It wasn't an iceberg. As I peered through the floating snowflakes, I saw that it was just a piece of frozen lake or river or whatever.

But why were there pieces of frozen lakes or rivers or whatever in the middle of May?!

More important, why had it started snowing?!

I threw open the window to see better and was hit by a gust of arctic air. I stuck out my head and looked up and down the street. Everywhere water pipes were bursting and fire hydrants were exploding—the water barely shooting out before it hardened into frozen fountains of ice.

I spotted our mailman floating by trying to catch the letters drifting out of his pouch.

"What's going on?!" I shouted.

"It's the s-s-sun!" he said with his teeth chattering. "It's getting s-s-smaller."

"That's impossible!" I cried. But even as I looked up at it, I could see the sun was shrinking. And the more it shrank, the colder it got.

Colder and darker!!

"Wally?" my little sister yelled from the porch below.

I glanced down at her. She was shivering worse than the postman. "I'm s-s-scared. M-m-make it s-s-stop!"

"I don't know how!" I yelled.

"It's b-b-because there's n-n-no gravity!" the mailman chattered.

I looked back at him. His face was turning blue and icicles were growing from his mustache.

He continued. "Without g-g-gravity, the earth c-c-c-an no longer c-c-circle the s-s-sun."

I turned back to the sun, watching as it continued to shrink. "You mean we're no longer orbiting the sun?!" I cried. "The whole planet is flying away?!"

"Without gravity, n-n-n-othing is h-h-holding it-t-t i-n-n-n p-p-la . . ." But he never finished the sentence.

I looked back at him and gasped.

The man had completely frozen! His eyes were open in a lifeless stare. His blue face was turning white from the frost and snow collecting on it!

In a panic, I yelled back to my sister. "Carrie, get inside! Get inside and shut the door before you—"

But I was too late.

She was already floating off the porch—her body growing stiff, her face turning blue.

"Carrie, NO!" I screamed. "CARRIE!"

I pushed myself out the window and kicked toward her, shivering so hard I thought my teeth would break. But that was my little sister out there. I had to get to her and help!

Other snow-covered bodies started drifting between us, their expressions also frozen.

All this as the sunlight continued to fade.

"C-C-CARRIE!" I fought my way through the cold, hard bodies. "C-C-C-C-CARRIE . . ."

At last I was able to grab her shoulders. When I spun her around I saw her frost-covered face—her mouth was frozen in a scream, and snowflakes were gathering on the lashes of her cold, lifeless eyes. Eyes frozen in terror.

But not only terror . . . accusation.

Accusation of me!

I jerked back and started tumbling away.

"DEAR GOD!" I shouted. I crashed into another frozen body. I turned until I was looking directly into the face of . . .

"DAD!"

But he gave no answer. His snow-covered face had the same lifeless expression as Carrie's, the same look of horror . . . and accusation!

Behind him floated my brothers.

"NO!" I shouted toward heaven. "YOU WERE RIGHT; I WAS WRONG. I WAS—"

I came to a stop as I saw another body floating toward me. It was hard to tell who, with the thick coating of frost. But the closer it came, the more terror I felt, until I finally recognized the hair. Though it was covered in snow, there was no mistaking it. It was hair that could only belong to:

"MOM!!!"

She'd come back! She'd come home! But she floated toward me with a face just as lifeless as the others. Her eyes frozen in the same terror and fear.

"NO!" I cried. "PLEASE, NOOO!"

I pushed away, tumbling head over heels out of control. "I DIDN'T KNOW! GOD, YOU WERE RIGHT! I DIDN'T KNOW!!"

I bumped into more bodies. All frozen. It was

too dark to see who they were. Too dark to see anything now. I felt the tears on my cheeks turning to ice, my own body stiffening, becoming harder and harder to move, tumbling and spinning and screaming:

"PLEASE . . . GOD, PLEASE, TAKE OVER . . . PLEASE . . . PLEASE . . ."

# Chapter 10

## Wrapping Up

"Wally . . . Wally, wake up . . ."

It almost sounded like Wall Street's voice, but it was too far away for me to be sure.

Another voice asked, "I hit him pretty hard. Is he going to be all right?"

"Sure." The first voice started getting louder. "In fact, if you've got twenty bucks, I'll let you hit him again."

(Yup, that was definitely Wall Street.)

It took all my effort to pry open my eyes (frozen eyelids can be a little hard to open). When I finally succeeded, I saw that the sun had come back!

All right!

In my excitement, I tried sitting up—but the pain shooting through my chest suggested I'd better get a couple of new ribs first.

Wait a minute . . . *PAIN*? I was feeling pain? How cool was that?!

"Hey, Wally, *burp,* you going to be okay?"

I turned toward fumes that smelled a lot like Chippy Chipper potato chips and, sure enough, there was Opera staring down at me! And it was the *old* Opera! Not the three-thousand-pound Opera! Not the mean, bully Opera! Just the good ol' Vice President of Dorkoids Anonymous

*BURP*

Opera.

"What happened?" I asked. "Where am I?"

"Soccer tryouts," Wall Street explained. "You got hit kinda hard by Sophie here."

I turned to see Sophie Stompuregut staring down at me with a bunch of the other kids from the school team.

"You're back," I croaked.

"From where?" she asked.

"From teaching coloring to preschoolers."

"What are you talking about?"

"Don't you remember?" I asked. "When I became the world's greatest soccer player, you quit playing because—"

"Whoa, whoa, whoa." Suddenly, her hands were on her hips with that supercompetitive look in her eyes. "Since when did you become a better soccer player than me?"

"Since my overactive imagination imagined I was." Then the entire team broke out laughing, including Coach Hurtumuch.

"I gotta tell you, McDoogle," he said, "only you'd have a big enough imagination to come up with that one."

"You mean I didn't become a major soccer pro?" I asked.

Repeat in the laughter department.

"You mean I'm not one of the richest guys in the world?"

"Not yet," Wall Street said, shrugging, "but if you stick with me, it's bound to happen . . . at least for one of us."

I lifted my head and looked around. "So what exactly happened?"

"You just had one of your McDoogle mishaps, that's all," Wall Street said. "You've been unconscious for the last four or five minutes."

"You mean nothing's changed?" I asked.

"Nothing except the time you've wasted lying around on my field," Coach Hurtumuch said.

I closed my eyes. Was it possible? Had it all been a dream? If that was true, then everything was back to normal—me, my family, my friends, the world . . .

"Do you think you can stand?" Wall Street asked.

I nodded as she and Opera helped me to my feet.

I still couldn't believe it, and I was still a little suspicious. Maybe my overactive imagination was being even more overly imaginative.

"Listen," Wall Street whispered to me. "Hurry up and get better. I got people willing to pay good money to see you get creamed again."

No, that was too real to be my imagination. It had to be just normal, everyday Wall Street living in my normal, everyday reality.

And so, as the rest of the soccer team returned to their tryouts, my two best friends carried me off the field and plopped me safely on the end of the players' bench.

Well, they had planned to plop me safely on the end of the players' bench. It wasn't their fault that the opposite end shot up into the air.

And you really couldn't blame them that the team's water cooler had been placed on that end.

Yes sir, it was poetry in motion, watching that water cooler sail high into the air, gracefully reaching its height and starting to plummet back down (ah, good ol' gravity) until it—"Wally, look out!"—

*K-Thudd*ed

ever so ungently onto my head, sending me back into the Land of Unconsciousness . . .

* * * * *

"So . . . ," a very familiar voice (that sounded a lot like my overactive imagination) asked, "did you learn your lesson?"

"Oh, no," I groaned, "you're back. What are you this time—a talking tree, a talking snail?"

"Oh, please," the voice said, "you've got a better imagination than that. I'm the pigeon poop beside your head as you're lying unconscious on the field."

I started to open my eyes, but he said, "Don't bother, this will be a short visit."

"You made all this up, didn't you?" I asked my overactive imagination. "Me being a superstar, being super-rich, creating a world with no pain, no gravity . . . all of it."

"Not bad, if I do say so myself," he said. "Now, have you finally learned your lesson?"

"Yeah," I said, nodding. "I think so."

"You *think* so. Well, if you're not sure . . ."

Suddenly, it got very dark and cold. I felt myself lifting off the field.

"No!" I cried. "I'm sure, I'm sure! You made your point! You made your point!"

"Very good," he said. Once again it got brighter and warmer . . . and I did my usual

"AUGH!"
*K-Rash*
"Oaff!"

slamming-into-the-ground routine.

But it was true. I meant what I said . . .

Even when it doesn't make sense to me, I have to remember that God has a plan. It may not be the plan I want . . . but it will *always* be better.

"Well, then," the pigeon poop said, "if you really believe it, then I guess my job is done."

"Not so fast," I argued. "What about the super-hero story?"

"Oh, you mean Pudgy Boy?"

"That's right. We still haven't had the big showdown with Boney Boy. And we can't have a superhero story without a superhero showdown."

"But you don't have Ol' Betsy," he said.

"I don't need her—not with my overactive imagination. But we have to hurry and do it before I wake up."

"Well, all right then," he said. "What are we waiting for? Let's get on with it!"

I nodded, took a moment to change gears, and . . .

Pudgy Boy slams on the brakes, bringing the Blubbermobile to a somewhat startling and

*SCREECHing*

halt at the base of a craggy mountain.

"And why a craggy mountain?" you ask.

(You are asking, right?)

Because at the top of that craggy mountain our hero just happens to spot a giant TV antenna perfect for broadcasting sinister, brain-changing signals. (Now you know why they pay him the big superhero bucks.)

Quickly, he leaps out of his car, straps on his rocket belt, and

*K-WHOOSH*

fires it up.

The only problem is, since he lost all that tonnage at Alkaflab Prison, the belt fits too loosely and takes off, leaving him behind!

But, thanks to some very fast thinking (and great work by an overactive imagination), he reaches in and pulls out the used dental floss he carries in his pocket for just such occasions.

He quickly makes a lasso out of it, and

*whip, whip, whips*

it around his head until he

*K-flings*

it into the air and snags the rocket belt. Of course, the belt is so power-ful that it

**YANKS**
"Ahhhhhhhhh..."

him up and away so that he sails over Boney Boy's headquarters, where he releases the floss and

**"Ahhhhhhhhh..."**
*K-Thuds*

smack-dab in front of Boney Boy and his Brain Wave transmitter. (Hey, I told you it was a good imagination.)

"Give it up, Boney Boy!" our hero shouts as he staggers to his feet.

"Never!" the not-so-nice guy replies not so nicely.

"Why?"

"Why?? What type of question is that? Because I'm the not-so-nice guy, of course."

"There must be another reason."

"There is no other reason...well, other than the fact that I woke up one morning and my jeans were too tight."

His bottom lip begins to quiver.

"That is when I realized I was, *sniff,* putting on..." He closes his eyes, trying to regain his composure. "That's when I realized I was putting on...**weight!**"

Suddenly, he bursts into uncontrollable tears.

"And from that moment on you hated the name Pudgy?" our hero asks.

Boney Boy nods, forcing out his words between sobs. "They were my favorite jeans, *sob.* And suddenly, *sob, sob,* overnight, *sob, sob, sob,* I was too fat to wear them!"

"Maybe it wasn't your fault."

"Of course it was my fault," the bad boy bawls, tears streaming down his skinny face. "And God was punishing me!"

"For what?"

"FOR EATING A WHOLE SIDE ORDER OF FRIES!" He drops to his knees, crying uncontrollably.

Our hero stoops down, trying his best to comfort him. "Maybe it was your mom's fault."

"FOR HAVING ME, YES!" he blurts. "YES! YES!"

"No, that's not what I meant. Maybe she just put your jeans in the dryer too long with the temperature set on High."

He looks up, blinking through his tears. "What?"

"Maybe your jeans just shrank."

"You mean..." He takes a ragged breath and tries again. "You mean maybe I'm not too fat after all?"

"We all need a little fat. It is only natural. In fact, some of us are actually built to be naturally heavier than others."

"That's terrible."

"No, it's natural...it's how God made us."

"Hey—you just worked the theme of this entire book into our little super-hero story!"

"I did?" (Wow, that overactive imagination really is good!)

"But," the bad boy bawls, "what about those skin-and-bones models I see in magazines and stuff?"

"I'm afraid some of them may be UNnatural. Some are so skinny it's actually unhealthy for them."

"But what about you?" he argues. "Eating all those pizzas and cake and—"

"You're right," our hero agrees, "I do need to be more careful with what I eat...and I need to exercise. But in moderation."

"*Moderation*...you mean doing some of the stuff, but not going overboard?"

"That's right."

"What an incredible concept!"

"Thanks. So are you going to turn off the Brain Wave machine?" our hero asks.

"With so few pages left in the book, I don't have a choice."

"I'm afraid you're right."

With that, the boney bad boy strolls over to the giant Brain Wave machine and reaches for the lever labeled:

**WARNING:**
*Shut off only when*
*story is about to end.*

But, just before he pulls it, he asks, "Are you going to cancel that pizza with extra caramel sauce and chocolate chip topping you ordered?"

"I've been waiting the entire story to get back to it!"

"You can still have the pizza, but what about a healthier topping?"

"What a cool idea."

"Thank you. I call it...moderation."

"But what can be healthier than caramel sauce covered with chocolate chips?" our hero asks.

"How about cauliflower smothered in broccoli sauce?"

"Hmm, sounds tasty."

"Well, that's one word for it."

"All right," our hero agrees, "it's a deal!"

And so, with that not-so-good-of-an-example of moderation (and before our good guy changes his mind about broccoli sauce topping), Boney Boy shuts down the Brain Wave machine.

And soon, after a moderate workout in the gym, the two stroll arm in arm into the sunset looking for the nearest health-food pizza place. Yes sir, it's another cornball ending as the sappy music swells and the credits roll...as all have learned the importance of accepting themselves the way they are made—while also watching what they eat and exercising in moderation.

Though still unconscious, I had to smile. I'd be waking up in a second or two. (I had to, the schmaltzy credit music was killing me.) And when I did, I'd make sure I'd be a bit more content with what I'd been given. And for the things I couldn't change . . . well, let's just say I'd be spending a bit more time thanking God and a little less time whining.

At least until my next major mishap.

thing can be explained rationally as he watches Denise struggle to grasp the enormity of the Imager's love. It's not until they meet the Weaver—who weaves the threads of God's plan into each life—that they both discover that understanding takes an element of faith.

Book 3: THE WHIRLWIND
(ISBN: 1-4003-0746-5)
The mysterious stone transports the three friends to Fayrah, where they find themselves caught between good and evil. There Josh falls under the spell of the trickster Illusionist and his henchman Bobok—who convince him that he can become perfect. Before they lose Josh in the Sea of Justice, Denise and Nathan must enlist the help of someone who is truly perfect. Will help come in time?

Book 4: THE TABLET
(ISBN: 1-4003-0747-3)
Denise finds a tablet with mysterious powers, and she is beguiled by the chance to fulfill her own desires—instead of trusting the Imager's plan. But when Josh and Nathan grasp the danger she faces, they work desperately to stop the Merchant of Emotions before he destroys Denise—and the whole world!